A Pony Named Shawney

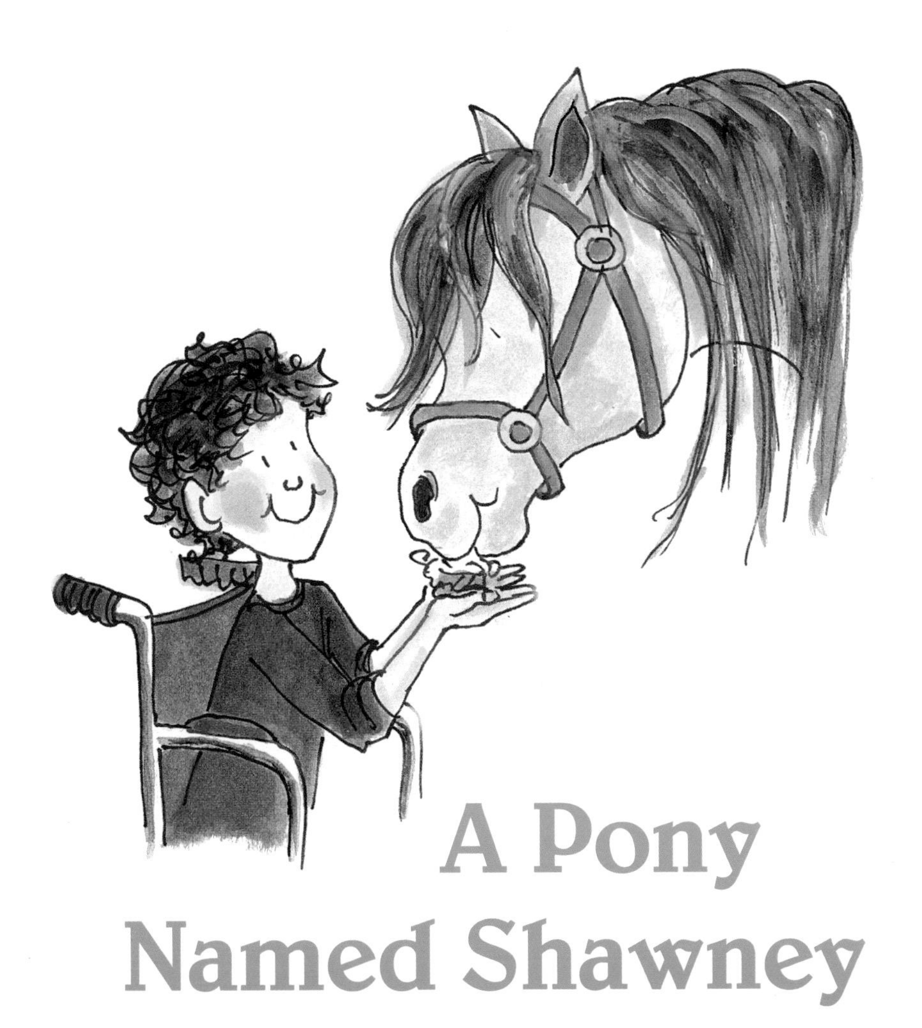

A Pony Named Shawney

by MARY SMALL

illustrated by SUÇIE STEVENSON

This edition first published in the United States of America in 1997 by
MONDO Publishing
Originally published as *And Alice Did the Walking*
By arrangement with MULTIMEDIA INTERNATIONAL (UK) LTD

For information contact:
MONDO Publishing, 980 Avenue of the Americas, New York, NY 10018

Printed in Hong Kong by South China Printing Co. (1988) Ltd.
First Mondo printing, July 1996
00 01 02 03 04 9 8 7 6 5 4

Original development by Robert Andersen & Associates and Snowball Educational
Design by Mina Greenstein
Production by Our House

Library of Congress Cataloging-in-Publication Data
Small, Mary.
A pony named Shawney / by Mary Small ; illustrated by Suçie Stevenson.
p. cm.
Summary: Seven-year-old Scott, who is physically handicapped, falls in love
with the neighbor's pony and dreams of having his own horse to do the walking
for him.
ISBN 1-57255-170-4 (paperback).
[1. Ponies—Fiction. 2. Physically handicapped—Fiction.]
I. Stevenson, Suçie, ill. II. Title.
PZ7.S6386Po 1996
[E]—dc20 95-43290
CIP
AC

Contents

A Pony Named Shawney

SCOTT HAD never thought about riding a pony — until he met Shawney.

All through the long, wet winter, the big field at the end of the garden lay empty. Only the birds flew there to search for grubs. The field belonged to the Old House next door to Scott's home. Then, after school one day, Scott saw Shawney standing there close to the fence.

She was the prettiest pony he had ever seen, a soft smoky-gray color with a thick, shaggy mane and a tail so long it almost brushed the ground. As Scott came close, she peered at him inquisitively with gentle brown eyes and nickered a friendly greeting. He knew her name was Shawney because it was written in bold red letters on the rug she was wearing. It seemed just the right name for her.

"Shawney," he called, and she thrust her soft muzzle through the wire towards his outstretched hand.

"Don't touch her!" Scott turned to see his mother walking towards him. "You have to be careful with ponies. Sometimes they kick or bite," she said. "She's not yours, so you'd better leave her alone."

Next morning, Shawney was still in the field, and she was there again in the

afternoon when Scott came home from school. She was there the next day and the next, always waiting at the fence, ears pricked up hopefully.

She already knew Scott would throw her bread when nobody was looking. It was good, tasty bread. Scott's father was the town baker, and in Scott's home there was always the warm, fresh smell of baking bread from the bakery next door.

On Saturday, when Scott was talking to Shawney through the fence, three children appeared at the far end of the field.

"Shawney! Come on, Shawney!" they called.

With an excited whinny and a toss of her head, the pony turned away from Scott and trotted off briskly.

Scott watched a little enviously as the children stroked the pony and fed her carrots. Then they put a bridle on her and led her away, out of sight.

For a long time Scott sat staring after them.

If only I had a pony like Shawney, she could do the walking for me, he thought.

Scott was unable to walk. Often people felt sorry for him, but mostly he didn't mind so much. He had never known what it felt like to

be able to walk. Scott could just manage to get around on a pair of crutches, but very slowly. He spent most of his time in his wheelchair. It was nearly as good as a car! He could go almost anywhere in it, as long as he avoided loose stones, curbs, and steps. He had lost count of how many times the wheelchair had run away with him, helter-skelter, and tipped him out onto the ground. But except for scratches and bruises, he was never hurt.

"The boy's made of rubber," his father said. "He'll never learn to be careful enough. All the same, he's got plenty of guts."

New Neighbors

ON SUNDAY, Scott wheeled himself up to the fence, as usual. He hoped he would see Shawney again.

There she was — with the three children. One of the boys was sitting on the pony. The girl was leading Shawney by the bridle. They passed by quite close to Scott, but the boys took no notice of him. The girl looked right at

him, but she didn't smile. Then they went off to the far end of the field.

Scott felt sad. He would have liked to say "Hello." Perhaps the children had felt awkward because he was in a wheelchair. Perhaps they felt they shouldn't stare at him.

When he got home, Scott asked his mother, "Who does Shawney belong to?"

"Shawney?" she asked. "Oh, you mean that little pony. She must belong to the new family who have come to live in the Old House. The letter carrier told me there are three children there at the moment. We might visit them. Would you like that?"

Scott wasn't sure. He remembered the girl's unsmiling glance and the way the boys hadn't looked at him at all.

Next day, after school, Shawney was back at the fence looking for Scott. She whinnied a greeting and took the piece of bread he held out for her.

"Scott!"

He turned and saw his mother behind him.

"It's all right, Mom," he said. "See! If

I hold my hand flat and put the bread on it, she can't bite my fingers, even by mistake."

"Maybe, but bread isn't really good for ponies, Scott," his mother told him.

"I didn't know that," Scott said. "I won't give her any more. I'll just talk to her."

"All right, but be careful," his mother said.

"Oh, Shawney," Scott whispered when his mother had gone, "I wish I could get on your back and ride you. Think of having four strong legs to walk with, instead of two useless ones."

Scott Thinks of a Plan

THE DAY after that, Scott went again to the field fence.

"It's just talking now, no bread to eat," he told Shawney.

But "just talking" didn't suit Shawney at all. When Scott put out his hand to pat her, she turned away. But she watched him while she grazed a little distance away, just in case he had some bread after all.

Scott could tell Shawney was losing interest in him. Each day after that, she was a little bit farther away from the fence.

Then Scott made a plan. On Saturday, when his mother was out shopping, he took several pieces of bread from the kitchen. He quickly wheeled himself out of the house, across the yard, under the clothesline, and up to the fence. He spied Shawney in the corner of the field, dozing.

"Shawney! Come on, Shawney!"

Scott held out the bread. Shawney came towards him at once, whinnying softly.

"Careful!" he said as she grabbed the bread. "Don't be so greedy."

He watched while Shawney ate the first piece of bread. Then, looking all around to make sure no one could see him, he set the brakes on his wheelchair and tipped himself out onto the ground.

SHAW

Shawney backed away as Scott dragged himself along the ground towards the fence, elbowing himself along on his tummy. He threw

her a second piece of bread, and as she ate it, he squeezed under the fence wire.

He lay there panting, looking up at the pony.

"Here!" He held out another piece and she took it.

Shawney looked much bigger than usual from where Scott lay on the ground. Slowly, carefully, he edged nearer to her. She watched him warily, her nostrils flaring, her long tail swishing slowly.

The strap of Shawney's rug was now within Scott's reach, and he put up both hands to grab hold of it. Shawney, alarmed, stepped sideways, and Scott lost his hold and fell flat on his face.

"What on Earth are you doing?" a voice exclaimed.

Jodie Lends a Hand

SCOTT lifted his head. The girl stood there, staring down at him in amazement. Awkwardly, he tried to sit up.

"N-Nothing," he said miserably. He wished he could suddenly disappear down a rabbit hole.

Then the girl's expression changed from anger to embarrassment. She was looking at his leg braces.

"Oh — I forgot. Can't you walk at all?" she asked in a voice not much louder than a whisper.

"No," said Scott, "but I don't mind. Not really. I don't even know what it feels like to be able to walk." He looked at the girl's sturdy legs. "What *does* it feel like?" he asked.

"I don't know — just like — walking, I suppose," the girl said, shrugging her shoulders.

Suddenly she dropped to the ground beside Scott, pulled up a piece of grass, and chewed it thoughtfully. "Isn't it awful not being able to walk?" she asked.

"A little bit awful," Scott said, "but I don't think about it all that much. At school I do exercises that make my legs stronger. One day I may be able to walk with crutches.

But I can go most places in my wheelchair."

The girl looked at the wheelchair, standing empty on the other side of the fence.

"My name's Jodie," she said. "Jodie McBain."

"Mine's Scott Anderson."

"How old are you?"

"Seven."

"I'm nine, nearly ten," Jodie told him. "We've come here from Maine. Mom likes the weather better here in Massachusettts."

"Who were those two boys with you the other day?" Scott asked.

"My cousins Michael and Roger. They've gone home now. They were only staying with us. I do have a brother, Russ, but he's a lot older than me." Jodie paused, and then she asked, "What were you trying to do just now?"

"I wanted to...to try to get on Shawney's back, just to see if she would do the walking for me," Scott said. "But she wouldn't stand still."

"Shawney is very old," Jodie said. "She's twenty-three. We've had her for years and years. But she's still lively." Jodie thought for a moment. Then she said slowly, "Would you really like to ride Shawney?"

"Oh yes!" said Scott. Then he added, "I don't know if Mom and Dad would let me though. That's why I tried to get on Shawney while they weren't home. Mom doesn't seem to like ponies much."

"I'll ask my Dad about it...about riding Shawney, I mean," Jodie said. "Maybe it will help if he talks to your parents."

Jodie got up.

"Can you get home all right?" she asked him.

"Yes."

"Okay. See you later."

Why Not Try?

SCOTT'S MOTHER noticed his muddy clothes when she came home from shopping, but she didn't ask any questions. She just said, "Oh, Scott! You fell out of your wheelchair again!"

Scott smiled to himself. He had decided to keep his adventure a secret and wait to see if Jodie's father came to talk to his parents. He felt pretty excited inside, all the same.

That evening, just as everyone sat down to dinner, there was a knock at the door. Scott's father opened it. A stranger stood there, with Jodie beside him.

"Does Scott live here?" the man asked.

Scott's mother got up from the table. "That's right. This is my son, Scott." She laid a hand on Scott's shoulder.

"Let me introduce myself. I'm your new neighbor, Ivor McBain. This is my daughter, Jodie, and out there in the driveway is my son, Russ, with Shawney."

Scott leaned forward in his chair and glimpsed a tall boy standing outside with the pony. He glanced at Jodie and she grinned at him.

"I understand from Jodie that Scott would like to ride," Mr. McBain said. "That's why we've brought Shawney with us."

"Ride!" Scott's mother gasped. "Ride Shawney? Wherever did you get that idea?"

Everyone looked at Scott. He took a deep breath. "If...if somebody lifted me up onto Shawney, I'm sure I could stay on," he said, sounding as confident as he could. He looked at his father. "Please let me try, Dad."

"It's not impossible," Jodie's father said. "These days, quite a lot of physically challenged children learn to ride."

"Shawney is only little," Scott pointed out. "Please Mom! Please Dad! You know how strong my arms are from working the wheelchair. And the teachers at school say the more exercise I get, the better."

His mother and father looked at each other.

"Well, I don't see why not," said Mr. Anderson. "If he falls off, he'll bounce. I've always said he's made of rubber!" Mr. Anderson lifted his son from his wheelchair and carried him outside to Shawney and Russ.

"Hi!" said Russ.

Very carefully, Mr. Anderson lifted Scott into the saddle. Scott grabbed the front of the saddle for safety. He felt very high off the ground.

"Put this riding hat on," Jodie said. "And we'll shorten the stirrups. Stand still, Shawney."

"You look fine," said Russ, smiling at Scott. "How does it feel?"

"Great!" said Scott. "Can we go for a ride now?"

"Sure. Just keep a tight hold on the front of the saddle, and we'll see that Shawney behaves. Another time we'll teach you how to hold the reins."

With Russ walking on one side and Mr.

McBain on the other, Jodie took the reins. She led Shawney up and down the backyard, very slowly, so that Scott could get used to the pony's movement. It was very strange to feel Shawney's warm, strong body moving beneath him and to watch her head move up and down in front. Once or twice Shawney stopped suddenly, and Scott fell forward onto her thick, wiry mane.

"I think that's enough," said Mr. McBain, "at least for today. We'll do this again very soon. Maybe next weekend."

Scott's body ached that night and his head spun with excitement. For a long time he lay in bed unable to sleep, thinking of Shawney and his ride and all the wonderful things they would do one day. At last he fell asleep dreaming of ranchers and open fields and fast, galloping horses.

Shawney Does the Walking

FROM THAT TIME ON, Saturday afternoons never came around quickly enough for Scott. For that was when Mr. McBain or Russ, and always Jodie, came with Shawney to teach Scott to ride.

After only a few lessons Scott felt less unbalanced and found he could sit up much straighter without trying so hard. He could even let go of the saddle and hold onto the reins, but he still held Shawney's thick mane as well, for safety. Somehow, Shawney seemed to know that riding was not easy for Scott. She always walked along quietly, but Scott still needed someone to walk by his side. If they turned a corner too sharply, he could lose his balance and fall off.

"When can we trot?" he asked Russ one day as they come back along the grass beside the road.

"Now, if you like," Russ said, "but you'll have to shorten the reins. Gather them up and push into the saddle with your body so Shawney knows you want her to move faster."

Scott got ready. Then Russ slapped Shawney on the rump and made "giddy-up" noises. The pony broke into a trot.

"Oh, stop! Stop!" cried Scott, grabbing wildly at Shawney's mane as he found himself bumping out of control.

"Whoa, Shawney!" called Russ, slowing the pony to a walk. "Maybe we'll leave the trotting for a while," he said. "You'll manage it, but not just yet. You need more practice at walking first."

When Scott had been riding for several weeks, his legs began to feel just a little stronger. If he held on to a table or chair, he could pull himself up and stand for a while on his own.

Then it was Christmas, and the long winter vacation began. And suddenly everything started to go wrong.

"We're off to Virginia for vacation," Jodie announced one day. "And we'll be taking Shawney. We're going to stay with my aunt and uncle and Michael and Roger."

Scott stared at her. "Going to Virginia! For how long?"

"The whole vacation. But you'll be able to ride again when we get back."

Scott thought winter vacation would never end. The days dragged on. He missed Shawney dreadfully. His parents took him to the movies or for drives in the country, but it wasn't the same as riding Shawney. Often Scott went to look in the field, hoping the McBains might have come home early from their trip. But only a mob of sheep grazed there, pulling at the dry, yellowing grass with quick, sharp bites. As soon as Scott came close they hurried away to a safe

distance to stand and stare at him. Each morning he woke to the sound of their baa-ing and bleating instead of the whinnying of a pony.

When Scott talked about Shawney at home, saying how much he missed her, his father would just smile, wink across to his mother, and say, "Never mind, son. You'll soon be riding again. Be patient."

Sometimes, lying in bed at night, Scott would listen to the old roof creaking and think enviously of Michael and Roger, Jodie's cousins, riding Shawney in Virginia. When at last he fell asleep, he saw Shawney in his dreams, but he could never quite reach her.

A New Pony

FINALLY, the weeks passed. Winter vacation was over, and it was time to go back to school. And still Shawney had not returned.

One evening, as Scott sat in his wheelchair watching television, there was a loud knock at the door. His mother went to answer it. He heard the sounds of whispering and muffled laughter. The next moment she came hurrying into the room.

"I think you'd better come outside." She pushed Scott along the passage to the front door. And there, standing in the yard, was Scott's father, all the McBains, and Shawney!

But was it Shawney? Surely his eyes must be playing tricks on him, Scott thought. The pony seemed bigger than he remembered her, and a darker gray. He sat there staring at the pony, and the pony stared back at him, with equal interest, it seemed.

"Well, haven't you anything to say?" asked his father. "How do you like your new pony?"

Scott was speechless for a moment. "*My* pony? What do you mean, Dad? *My* pony? What about Shawney?"

"We left Shawney in Virginia with Jodie's cousins," Mrs. McBain said. "She's getting to be quite an old lady now. So we looked around for another pony and found Dusty. And

here he is! He's a present from your parents."

Scott looked at his mother and father, who stood there smiling.

"It wasn't easy to keep it all a secret," Scott's mother said.

"Dusty!" Scott echoed the name, still scarcely able to believe it was all true.

"He's only seven years old," said Jodie. "The same as you, Scott. It took us ages to find him. We knew you'd want a pony as much like Shawney as possible."

"Don't you want to meet him?" Scott's father asked.

"Oh, yes!" said Scott. Mr. McBain picked up Scott and took him over to Dusty, who nickered softly as Scott stroked his forehead.

Scott looked across at his mother and Mr. McBain.

"Does he really belong to me?"

"Head, tail, and all four legs!" his mother said.

"We're going to make a gate in the fence

and build a shelter shed for him in the field," said Mr. McBain. "Jodie will help you exercise him, and keep his saddle and bridle clean."

"Thanks! Thanks a lot!" was all Scott could say. But everybody standing around could see just how pleased and proud he felt to have a pony of his own. Now Dusty would do the walking for him, and that, as far as Scott was concerned, was just about the greatest thing in the world.

Author's Note

All around the world, children and adults who are challenged by limited sight, paralysis, or other conditions enjoy the fun and therapeutic benefits of riding horses. Riding for the Disabled is a worldwide organization that provides riding grounds, specially selected quiet ponies and horses, volunteer helpers, and qualified instructors. Medical approval to ride is essential.

MARY SMALL is a speech therapist who now writes full-time for children. Since 1974, she has been involved with the Riding for the Disabled Association in Australia and, since 1979, editor of *Riding Free*, the Association's national journal.

Born in England, Ms. Small emigrated to Australia in 1962. She now lives in Sydney.

SUÇIE STEVENSON is the illustrator of over 30 books for young readers, including the *Henry and Mudge* books by Cynthia Rylant, *Emily and Alice* and *Emily and Alice Again*, both by Joyce Champion, and *Baby-O* by Nancy White Carlstrom. Books she has both written and illustrated include *Christmas Eve*, *Jessica the Blue Streak*, *The Princess and the Pea*, and *The Emperor's New Clothes*.

Ms. Stevenson lives in Cape Cod, Massachussetts, with her two dogs, who sleep under her desk while she works.